2222222222222
3333333333333
4444444444444

2222222222222222

3333333333333

444444444444444

Donated by
Eden Park
PTO
2000

WHAT COMES IN

2's, 3's, & 4's?

By Suzanne Aker

Illustrated by Bernie Karlin

Aladdin Paperbacks

Aladdin Paperbacks
An imprint of Simon & Schuster
Children's Publishing Division
1230 Avenue of the Americas
New York, NY 10020
Text copyright © 1990 by Suzanne Aker
Illustrations copyright © 1990 by Bernie Karlin
Also available in a hardcover edition from Simon &
Schuster Books for Young Readers
Designed by Bernie Karlin
Printed in Hong Kong
10   9

Library of Congress Cataloging-in-Publication Data

Aker, Suzanne.

What comes in 2's, 3's and 4's?

Summary: Introduces the numbers two, three,
and four, by enumerating the ways in which they occur
in everyday life, from your two eyes and two arms
to the four seasons of the year.

1. Counting—Juvenile literature.   (1. Number concept.
2. Counting.)   I. Karlin, Bernie, ill.
II. Title.   III. Title: What comes in twos, threes, and fours?
QA113.A52   1990   (E)   89-35482
ISBN: 0-671-79247-4 (pbk)

WHAT COMES IN
2's, 3's, & 4's?

To my three grandsons,
Aaron, Anthony,
and Trent — S.A.

To my wife, Mati — B.K.

WHAT COMES IN 2's?

Just look at you!
You have
2 eyes,
2 ears,
2 arms,
2 hands,
2 legs,
and
2 feet.

And when you look in the mirror,

there are **2** of you.

There are **2** handles on the sink – one hot and one cold.

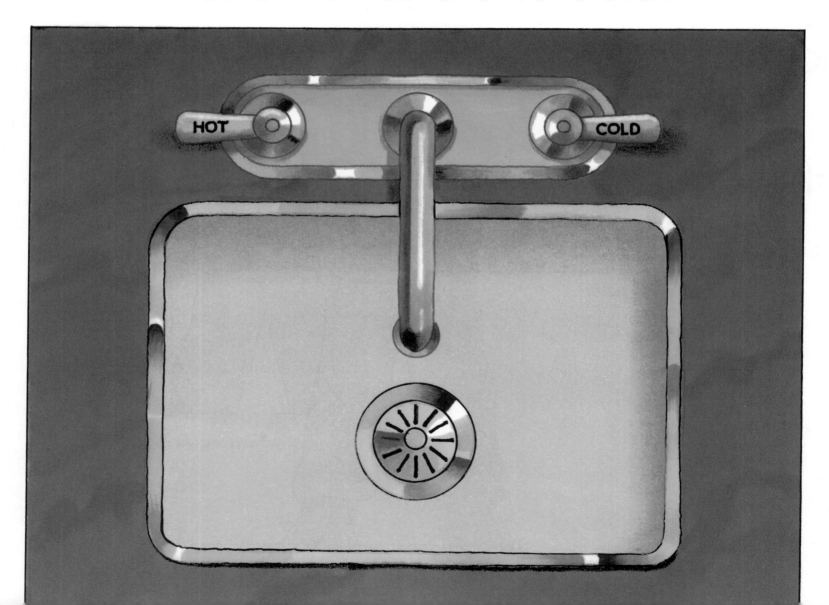

There are **2** pieces of bread on the sandwich.

There are
2 ways
to go on a
seesaw – up…

and down.

Birds
have
2 wings.

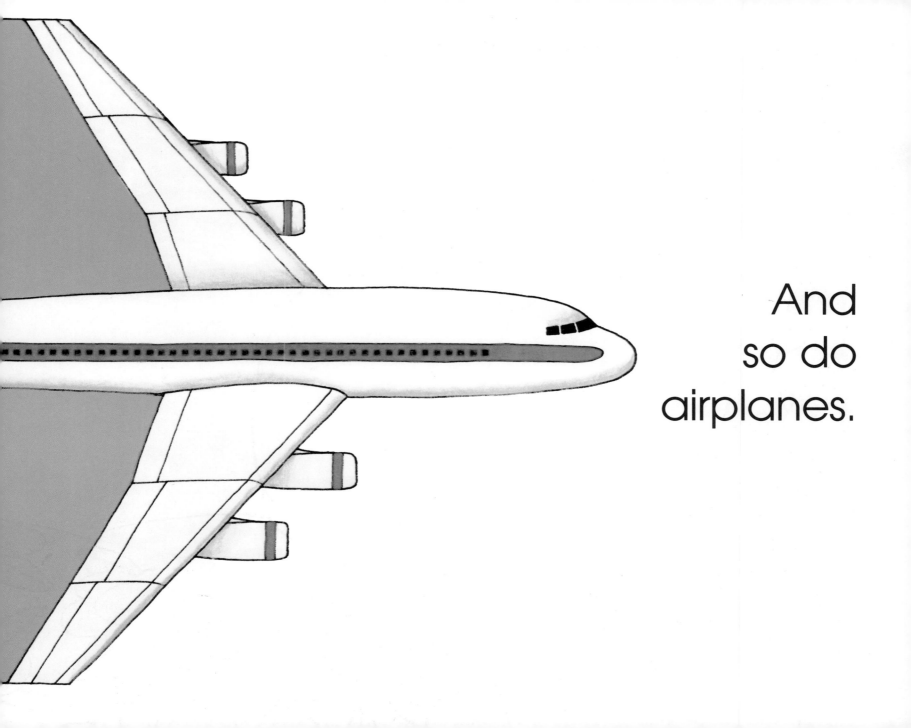

And
so do
airplanes.

There are **2** pillows on the bed.

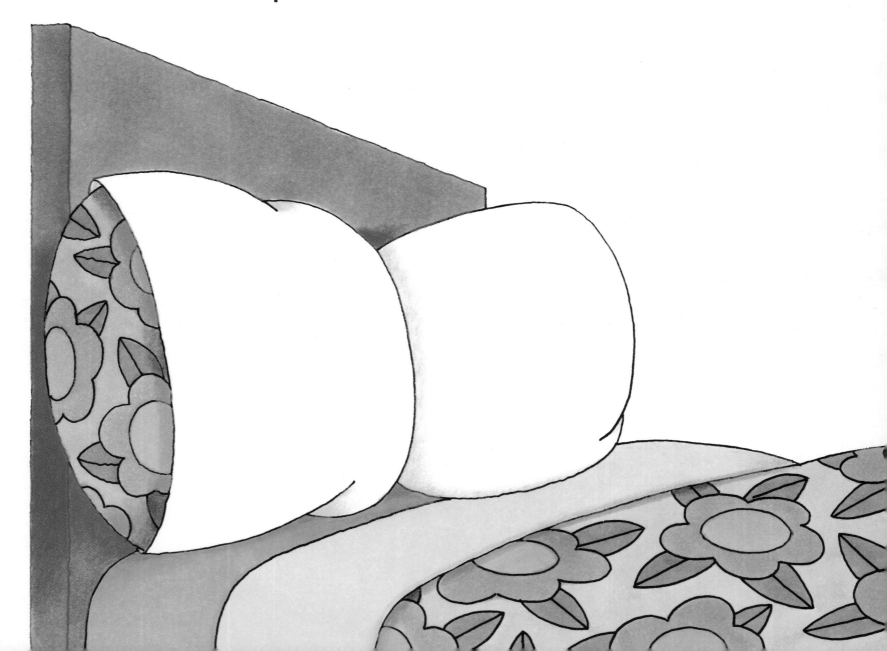

And **2** teddy bears waiting for you to say good night.

WHAT COMES IN 3's?

Traffic signals have
3 lights – red for stop,

yellow for slow,

and green for go.

There are **3** wheels on a tricycle.

We have **3** meals each day –
breakfast,   lunch,   and dinner.

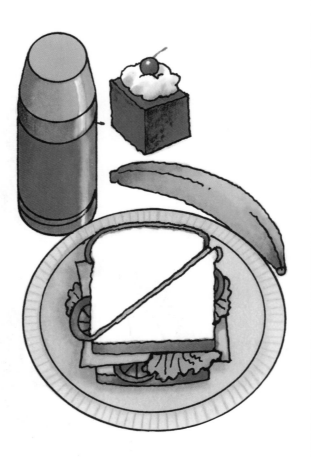

Here are **3** things that help us to eat –
a knife, a fork, and a spoon.

Most things come in **3** sizes –
small,   medium,   and large.

There are **3** colors you can mix
to make other colors –
red, yellow, and blue.

These are **3** important shapes –
a circle, a square,

and a  triangle.

There are **3** sides to a slice of pizza.

And **3** leaves on poison ivy —
watch out!

WHAT COMES IN 4's?

There are **4** wheels on mommy's car.

And **4** wheels on my wagon.

The chair has **4** legs and so does the table

So does the cat  and so does the dog.

There are
4 panes of glass
in the window.

And **4** places to cook on the stove.

There are **4** seasons in the year – spring,

summer, fall, winter

And there are
4 corners on this book.

Can you count them?

2222222222222

3333333333333

4444444444444

2222222222222

3333333333333

44444444444

A Day with Bonefish Joe

A Day with Bonefish Joe

by ELIZABETH HOWARD *with illustrations by* DIANA WEGE

David R. Godine · *Publisher*

BOSTON

Published in 2015 by
DAVID R. GODINE, *Publisher*
Post Office Box 450
Jaffrey, New Hampshire 03452
www.godine.com

LIBRARY OF CONGRESS CATALOGING-IN-PUBLICATION DATA
Howard, Elizabeth, 1950–
A day with Bonefish Joe / by Elizabeth Howard ;
illustrated by Diana Wege.
    pages cm
SUMMARY: Young Flossie is thrilled when she finally gets the chance
to spend a day at sea with Bonefish Joe, one of the best-known bonefish
guides in the Bahamas. Includes facts about Joseph Cleare and Harbour
Island.
ISBN 978-1-56792-534-0 (alk. paper)
[1. Fishing—Fiction. 2. Bahamas—Fiction.] I. Wege, Diana, illustrator.
II. Title.
PZ7.1.H687DAY 2015
[E]—dc23   2015000580

First edition

Dedicated to Bonefish Joe and Thomas Moorhead

Flossie fidgeted in her chair, counting the minutes until school let out. In her mind she was already running across the street and down the pier onto the Harbour Island dock.

Then she was there. She stepped around the suitcases and satchels, as music from the waiting taxis filled the air. Passengers were hugging hello and waving good-bye.

Flossie looked up at the big ferry deck and then she turned to see if she could spot Bonefish Joe returning from an afternoon of fishing in his small white boat.

Flossie was curious. More than curious.

Bonefish Joe was beloved by everyone. Visitors came on
yachts, on the ferry and in water taxis just to go fishing
with him. Why, Flossie wondered.

It was mysterious.

One afternoon while walking along the shore, Flossie
recognized Bonefish Joe in the distance. She stopped in
her tracks. Then, gathering all her courage, she waited
until Bonefish Joe was just in front of her. She looked up
and asked, "Bonefish Joe, would you take me out in your
boat and teach me to fish?"

Bonefish Joe's rugged frame shook with laughter.
"Miss Flossie, take a little girl out bonefishin'?"

Bonefish Joe's laughter was still in the air when he leaned down, placed his hands on her shoulders and said: "I'll take you out bonefishin' one day if your mama tells me it's O.K." Then he turned and walked on his way.

Flossie closed her eyes and took a deep breath.

She started running down Bay Street. Past Stillpoint with its yellow shutters. Past Doll House with its pretty pink shutters and bougainvillea flowers. Past Rosebud with its white picket fence and Loyalist Cottage. She turned up Princess Street and into Dunmore Town where her mother worked at Arthur's Bakery.

The screen door banged, napkins flew from the shelf
and everyone looked up when Flossie burst into Arthur's.
Breathlessly she blurted out: "Mama, Bonefish Joe will
take me bonefishing if you say 'yes.'"

"Catch your breath and slow down. Everyone's looking at you.
Come here and talk with me quietly," said her mother.

"Flossie, why would Bonefish Joe take a girl out bonefishing?
He only takes the people who come to Harbour Island on
the yachts and the water ferries. They pay him. Now, you run
along home and work on your homework. Stop with all this
silly imagining in your head."

Flossie didn't know what to think.

How could she do her homework? How could she sleep
when all she wanted to do was go fishing with Bonefish Joe?
When would her mother talk with Bonefish Joe?

Cock-a-doodle-doo!

It was Sunday, and it had been almost a week since Flossie had talked with Bonefish Joe. Every morning when she sat up in bed and began to rub the sleep from her eyes she wondered if today might be the day.

"Flossie," her mother called from the kitchen, "I talked with Bonefish Joe and I've decided to let you go bonefishing with him this afternoon. You can meet him at the dock after church. I want you to wear your red shorts and your sneakers."

Flossie clapped her hands with joy.

"Flossie, calm yourself down now. Finish your breakfast and then get dressed," her mother insisted.

Flossie's mother was wearing a green chiffon dress and a hat trimmed with satin ribbon bows, and was carrying an old family Bible when they left for church. Flossie was so excited she ran ahead.

Flossie's friends were in front of the church that was across the street from Dilly Dally's, smack in the center of town.

"Flossie, why are you wearing shorts?" one of them asked. "I'm going fishing with Bonefish Joe," Flossie told them. Not knowing whether to believe her or not, they just giggled. Why would Flossie want to go fishing anyway?

Flossie and her friends slipped into the church through the side door and found seats in the back pews, away from the stares of the grownups who were serious about their praying.

Ma Ruby was in the first row wearing a black and white polka-dot dress and the broadest hat covered with ribbon and lace Flossie had ever seen. Mama Sarah, the oldest lady on the island, was in the third row, wearing a blue sweater and a simple straw hat.

Soon the congregation was swaying to the music and raising their voices in prayer. There were readings of Psalms, more praying and what seemed like the longest sermon Flossie had ever heard. By the time the pastor's voice reached the back of the church with "Go in Peace. May the Lord bless you," Flossie was out the door.

The ferry was in, the water taxis were idling and Bonefish Joe was just pulling up to the dock as Flossie came running down the pier.

Bonefish Joe offered his hand and helped her down into the boat and onto one of the two small leather seats.

As they pulled away from the dock, the front of the boat rose up out of the water. Flossie could feel the wind against her face. Puffs of white clouds floated across the blue sky. When Flossie looked back across her shoulder all she could see was an outline of Harbour Island.

When they reached a cove Bonefish Joe stopped the engine
and pulled the motor up into the boat. The only sounds
were birds twittering, the waves splashing against the boat
and the gentle whisper of the breeze. The sun's reflection
sparkled like diamonds and danced across the water.

Leaning over the edge of the boat, they watched a sea turtle
move gracefully through the water.

"I see a starfish," Flossie exclaimed. As the boat drifted close
to the shore Flossie looked at the narrow sandy beach covered
with mottled rocks, shells and branches from the mangrove trees.

"Now we're goin' to the sandy flats lookin' for bonefish,"
said Bonefish Joe. With that he stood up, lifted the motor
back into the water and started the engine.

In the sandy flats they could see layers of ripples in the sand through the shallow water. Bonefish Joe began using a long pole to push the boat. It was mirror-still and Flossie could hear the drip, drip, drip of the water falling off the pole as Bonefish Joe dipped it in the water.

"Noise spooks the bonefish," Bonefish Joe whispered to Flossie. Then, in a barely audible voice, he began to sing.

> *Bonefish, bonefish, where are you?*
> *You must be on the sandy flats*
> *Or hiding in a cove.*
> *But, I'm a coming,*
> *Where you've been digging . . .*
> *Wiggle jiggin', wiggle jiggin'.*

Flossie sat silently listening to him until Bonefish Joe turned and handed her a fishing rod. "Just hold this until I tell you what to do. We'll cast the line out when we spot some bonefish."

"Flossie, stand up and try to cast a few times. Pull your arm back across your shoulder and let the line fly." Bonefish Joe's bare feet, callused from spending so much time in the water, kept him anchored to the boat, even as it moved through the water.

Flossie was still practicing when Bonefish Joe quietly said to her: "Stand up now and cast the line straight out." He raised the pole high in the air to show her. Flossie let the line fly out into the air. She watched until she could see the tan feathers at the end of the line disappear into the water.

Bonefish Joe kept his eyes on her line. "Flossie, slowly jig the line to the right . . . Stop . . . Jig it agin' . . . Reel . . . Reel . . . Slowly . . . Reel . . . Reel . . . Stop . . . Hold steady." Just then Flossie felt a tug on the line. The line pulled tighter . . . and tighter . . . and tighter . . . until Flossie could barely hold on.

That fish was fast and strong. What if the bonefish pulled her out of the boat?

"Bonefish Joe, he's swimming away."

"Let 'im run," Joe said calmly. "Hang on. Walk around the boat and keep the rod up as high as you can."

How could Flossie lift the rod when the fish was doing its best to pull it down?

The reel was making a loud whirring noise and the fleeing bonefish on the other end was pulling the line out faster and faster.

How long could this go on?

Bonefish Joe hadn't stopped talking. To Flossie. To the bonefish. To himself. Flossie couldn't quite understand what he was saying because she was trying to keep both her balance and the fish on the line.

"Now we'll pull 'im in." Bonefish Joe stood behind Flossie and wrapped his strong hands over her small fingers. They reeled . . . and reeled . . . and reeled until finally they could see the bonefish. Flossie couldn't believe her eyes.

When the bonefish was close to the boat, Bonefish Joe
scooped it into a net. "Bonefish Joe, the bonefish is so *small*.
How could it be so strong?" asked Flossie in amazement.

"Bonefish are the fastest and boniest fish in the water.
We catch 'em for the sport of it, the fun of it, and let 'em go.
Catch 'em and let 'em go," Bonefish Joe repeated and laughed.

Flossie sat down and started thinking about what she would
tell her friends.

Then Bonefish Joe kneeled down and, as gently as possible,
removed the hook and let the bonefish slide into the water.
They watched as its tail wiggled from side to side and it
swam away.

"Flossie, it's gettin' late and it's time to be goin' home,"
said Bonefish Joe.

He put the fishing rods and the pole down, stepped into the
water to push the boat into deeper water and then climbed
in and turned on the motor.

The sun was low in the sky as they traveled back to Harbour Island. When they arrived at the dock Bonefish Joe helped Flossie out of the boat and gave her a big hug.

"Flossie, you're learnin' real fast. You'll be quite a fisherwoman one day."

Flossie waved to Bonefish Joe as he pulled away from the dock.

Flossie's mind was filled with images of the giant sea turtle, the fluttering starfish, the silver bonefish and the sunlight dancing across the water. She could hear the sounds of the waves lapping against the boat, the drip, drip, drip of the water from the long pole and Bonefish Joe's laughing and singing.

Now she knew why people came to Harbour Island. It wasn't just for the fishing. Bonefish Joe took you by the hand and brought you to a peaceful and quiet place.

She knew she'd never forget her day with Bonefish Joe.

Joseph Cleare or "Bonefish Joe," as he was affectionately known on Harbour Island, was a legendary figure among those interested in the sport of bonefishing. He was recognized as much for his laughter and gentle manner as for his skill as a guide and patience as an instructor.

Harbour Island, only three miles long and half a mile wide, is one of the oldest settlements in the Bahamas and is best known for its broad pink-sand beach that runs the entire length of its Eastern shore. The streets, house names and personalities mentioned in the story are based on real people and places.